1/14/87

Dear David
   I hope you enjoy this
book. I love you as a
son. You really try hard
when you do something. I
like that you like to do
things with me.
            Love Dad

The Scary Basketball Player

The Scary
Basketball Player

by

Jerry B. Jenkins

MOODY PRESS

CHICAGO

ISBN: 0-8024-8233-3

2 3 4 5 6 Printing/LC/Year 90 89 88 87 86

Printed in the United States of America

To Dianna

Contents

1

The Announcement

It was hard for Jimmy Calabresi and me to get the rest of the Baker Street Sports Club settled down that late September afternoon. We were huddled in the chilly shed at the back of Mrs. Ferguson's farm where we met every day.

I had told everyone I had a big announcement, so all seven of us were there—Loren and Derek had moved just before school started, leaving our club with two fewer members.

I'm not sure the other six really thought my announcement would be anything important, though, because they were chattering away about the first week of school and everything.

Jimmy, my chubby, dark-haired best friend, finally got everyone's attention by slamming a hammer onto a license plate that had been nailed to a homemade table. What a racket! He shouted at the others. "Listen up! O'Neil hasn't even told *me* what he's gonna tell you, so be quiet!"

I hadn't really wanted to be the president of the club, but now that I had been for the first several months, I enjoyed it. We all got along real well, at least as well as you could hope with a bunch of guys almost the same age.

Jimmy joined the others, and they sat on the wood floor with their backs against the wall, their knees drawn up, and their hands clasped in front of them. Toby was the biggest, much taller even than Jimmy, but not so heavy. He was wide and thick and muscular, and he was a slow runner.

Also staring up at me was Bugsy, a slim, almost tiny black kid with huge eyes. He was probably the fastest runner in the club—after me—and afraid of nothing or no one. Next to him sat Ryan, a poor kid who didn't even have his own bike. He was like a white version of Bugsy though, almost the same size.

Sitting on the other side of Jimmy Calabresi was Cory the redhead. Crazy Cory we called him sometimes. He was loud and wild and the quickest one to argue, fight, yell, or cry. He did everything full blast. When we played baseball, he'd slide into *first* base. And every other base too, whether he needed to or not.

Then there was the quiet one, Brent. He had blond, almost white, hair. He was also small and fast and moved like a natural athlete.

As for me, I was average for a twelve-year-old, maybe a little taller than most. My hair was regular brown, and I was pretty good in sports, except I never thought I was as good as the rest of the guys said I was. They all thought I was the best in whatever sport we tried, but I never thought about it that much. I just enjoyed playing, especially with those guys.

Cory was fidgety. "Get on with it, Dallas. I gotta get home before dark."

I leaned back against the table, enjoying the delicious feeling that I had something to say that everyone would be thrilled about. "You know that Toboggan Road School still can't afford a basketball team."

Everybody nodded. Cory the redhead was still in a talking mood. "They haven't had any sports there since my dad graduated in sixty-five. So what?"

I ignored him. "You ever hear of the B.A.B.L.?"

"The B.A.B.L.? What's that?"

"The Boys Amateur Basketball League."

They had never heard of it. I hadn't either until I saw something in the sports page of the local paper, running a list of the standings from the year before and announcing the start of the new season. It was a league for boys eight through twelve, and it was sponsored by the Park City Recreational Department.

Before I could explain that I had already called the newspaper and got the phone number of the president of the league, Jimmy was ready with his objection. "Just like Little League. They're in Park City, and we're here in farm country. No way they'll let us play in their league."

But he was wrong. "It's not like that, Jimmy. This league is different. I talked to Mr. Bruce Lemke who started the league about six years ago. He says they play all their games, except their all-star games, which could be any-where, at Jefferson High in Park City. There are seven teams in the league, and they're looking for an eighth."

Cory was suspicious. "What's the catch?"

"No catch, but it *will* cost us."

"Cost us what?"

I hesitated, wondering how badly the guys wanted to form a team and play in a league. "Well, we have to have a coach, and we have to raise two hundred dollars for an entry fee, and we have to provide our own uniforms."

Big Toby sat scowling. "That's almost thirty bucks a guy. What's it for?"

"Insurance. Rent on the gym at Jefferson. Referees. Basketballs. Nets. Stuff like that. But Toby, and all you guys, listen: that's just for the entry fee. Mr. Lemke prom-ised he wouldn't break us up and put us on different teams like they do in Little League. As long as we prove we are no older than twelve and no younger than eight, we can enter as a team. But we have to have uniforms acceptable to the B.A.B.L."

"What's that mean?"

"They have to be more than just tee shirts. They have to be real uniforms from the shoes and socks on up."

"How're we supposed to get those?"

"That's our problem."

"How much are they?"

"He told me what companies make the kinds of uniforms that would be approved by the league, and I got a couple of catalogs at the sporting goods store. They're not cheap."

Ryan shook his head and spoke quietly. "No way. Forget it. I can't play."

I knew what he meant. We were all country people without extra money. (Jimmy's dad was the only one who even wore a suit to work.) But Ryan didn't have a father, and he had two older brothers and two younger sisters. He wore the same clothes almost everyday. There was no way his mother was going to be able to come up with the registration money, let alone a basketball uniform and shoes that would probably total twice as much as the fee.

But I wanted to know if the guys were interested. "We're a sports club. We had a good baseball season. We're supposed to be interested in all sports. There are no school sports for us, we can't join Little League, and we've got a chance here for some real competition with kids our own age. I have a plan for how we might be able to pull this off, but I have to know if you're all with me or not. No way we can do it with less than seven guys, so if anybody wants out, we'll forget it now."

Ryan raised a hand. "No money. Sorry. I'd love to, but—"

I smiled. "You'd love to, fine. That's all I need to hear. Jimmy?"

"Sure, but—"

"OK, Brent?"

"Yeah. But—"

"Good, Bugsy?"

"I guess you're not allowin' any argument, so count me in. It'll take a miracle to raise that much—"

"OK, Toby?"

Toby shrugged. "I don't know how you're gonna—"

"In or out, Toby?"

"In, I guess, but—"

"OK, Cory?"

"No!"

"No?"

"No! Forget it! I haven't got that kind of money, and I don't know anybody who does. You're not gonna get that rich kid friend of your mother's to buy us uniforms again are you, because as nice as that was, I don't want some city kid thinkin' I need charity."

I was afraid of that. "But Cory, listen. All I need to know is, if I find a way we can afford it, will you be on the team?"

"Sure, but—"

"That's all I needed to know."

"No, it isn't, O'Neil." Cory stood and his red hair was flying. "I told you I'm not takin' no charity, and that's that, all right?"

"All right! Sit down. We're going to raise all the money ourselves. We're going to do whatever we have to do—sell stuff, rake leaves, clean out garages and basements, anything. We'll work hard, put all the money in one place, and keep track until we have enough."

"How much is enough?"

We looked at the catalogs, and it was amazing how quickly everybody got excited about joining the league. Just looking at the pictures of our favorite pro stars running up and down the court in great uniforms made us dream of how we'd look in them.

Even the cheapest uniforms acceptable to the Boys Amateur Basketball League were seventy dollars each, including tax and postage. I knew it sounded like a lot. "With the registration fee, it looks to me like we need to raise about a hundred dollars each."

Cory leaned over the catalog. "How long will it take 'em to make our uniforms?"

I read the ordering page. "Four weeks."

"And when is the first game of the B.A. whatever you called it?"

"The B.A.B.L. The Boys Amateur Basketball League. Just over a month away."

"That means we'd have to order them now."

"So give me your shirt and waist and shoe sizes."

"But, Dallas, if we order 'em now, we'll have to pay for 'em even if we don't raise the money."

"Right."

There was a big sigh, from a total of six other guys. And I knew I was going to have to tell them a little about what faith meant. "You want to play in this league or not?"

"Well, yeah, but—"

"That attitude's not going to get us into the league. We've got another twenty minutes till dark. Let's talk. If I can't convince you we can do it, we'll just forget it."

2
The Hayloft

My Baker Street Sports Club friends knew I was a Christian, and they put up with my praying and even reading the Bible to them sometimes. They liked the stories I told them from the Bible, but I couldn't talk them into coming to church with me, even though I tried to tell them that that was where I heard most of my Bible stories.

That night I told them two stories. The first was about Nehemiah and how he built the city walls against all odds. Then I told them about Gideon and how he and a tiny band of men conquered a huge enemy just by obeying God.

Jimmy, even though he was my best friend, was sarcastic. "So, Pastor O'Neil, what's God telling us to do?"

"I'm not saying He's telling you to do anything, but I do know that if we do what's right, and if we work hard and stick together, there isn't much we can't do."

Bugsy spoke up. "We want to play in that league, Dallas. At least I do."

The others chimed in. "Me too. Me too."

"Then we're going to have to get busy and figure out how we can earn some money. The first thing we have to do is put in whatever extra money we've saved from our allowances and birthday gifts and stuff like that."

Ryan frowned. "I don't even *get* an allowance."

I wanted to assure him that we didn't care. "That's all

right. I think we should put all our money into a box without anyone knowing how much anyone else put in. Then we'll count it and see how much farther we have to go. Then we'll tell our parents we'll do whatever they want so we can earn extra money, then we'll try our neighbors, teachers, relatives, everyone."

"Should we tell 'em why we want to earn money?"

"Not unless they ask. Unless you want to. It wouldn't hurt anything."

Toby was still troubled. "Where are we gonna practice, Dallas? You and Jimmy are the only ones with hoops, but your driveways aren't smooth. The ball bounces all over the place. And your rims aren't the right height, are they?"

I admitted mine wasn't. "Just over eight feet."

Jimmy shook his head. "Mine's over nine, but not ten like it's supposed to be. I s'pose I could get my dad to raise it, but I'd still have the gravel driveway. Doesn't Mrs. Ferguson have a hoop up in the hayloft of that old gray barn of hers, down by the creek?"

I hadn't ever been in there. "In the hayloft?"

Jimmy was certain. "Yeah, we'd have to clean that out, but my dad and I have played in there before. It's dark. The only light comes from the swinging door over the haymow, and it smells like, like, you know—"

I smiled. "Like an old barn."

Jimmy laughed. "It's worth checking, anyway. If it's the right height, maybe we can draw some lines and see how big a court we can make. Maybe we can get a half-court out of it. At least a regulation size free throw lane."

The next day during my study period, I wrote up the order for seven basketball uniforms and seven pairs of shoes and socks. I chose colors that matched the baseball uniforms that Rodney Blasingame had bought for us.

The basketball uniforms had white shoes with blue stripes, white socks with blue and red stripes at the top, and white shorts and shirts with blue and red piping with big blue numbers edged in red.

He's got a secret weapon this year, too, he tells me. A big center."

"How big?"

"He won't say, and I haven't seen the boy yet, so I couldn't tell you. I suppose you'll find out soon enough, huh?"

"Yes, sir. How big are most of the centers in this league?"

"Oh, we've got a couple who might be close to five-ten."

"Five-*ten*?!"

"Yeah. Not so big, really. Well, sort of, I guess, for twelve-year-olds. How big is your center?"

I didn't know. "Well, we haven't really decided on starters yet, but our biggest player would be a kid named Toby, and he's about five-eight."

"Hm."

"Too small?"

"Well, if he's your biggest, I suppose you have a lot of speed."

"Oh, yes. We do. I'd say three of our guys are pretty fast." I was thinking that neither Toby or Jimmy were any too quick, but the rest of the whole club was fast, regardless who started.

Mr. Lemke sure seemed nice, and I was eager for them to meet him and have him meet our team.

Jimmy and I talked to Mrs. Ferguson and took a look at the hoop she had up in the hayloft. She hadn't even remembered it was there. "If it's there, you can certainly use it, and yes, you can clean the hay out. In fact, you'd have to, because I think it's almost wall to wall and floor to ceiling by now."

She was right. We had to climb a makeshift ladder next to an old wagon. Jimmy could hardly squeeze between the wagon and the wall, and as we moved hand over hand up the wood slats nailed to the barn studs, we were met by an eight-foot high stack of hay.

We scrambled to the top of it and found the basketball hoop. It was old and rusted and cracked, and there was no

15

net. And though it was two feet above the top of the hay, we couldn't be sure it was exactly ten feet until we cleared out the loft and measured.

Even if it was, we couldn't afford a net just then, and the nets on Jimmy's and my rims were already hanging in shreds. The big problem would be lighting. We would do most of our practicing after dark, and there was just one light in the place. It was high up at the peak of the roof.

I tried the switch. Nothing. "Best we can do is put the biggest bulb we can find up there."

Jimmy looked overwhelmed. "We've got an awful lot of work to do, Dal. An awful lot."

3
Raising the Money

O ver the next three weeks, no kids anywhere had a schedule like the Baker Street Sports Club. We were trying to get used to new grades, new teachers, new classmates, more homework, harder subjects, and all kinds of stuff.

But that wasn't all. We got permission to work between the end of school and when it got dark, promising our parents we would do homework right after supper. Then, if there was another hour or so before bedtime, we worked on clearing the hayloft.

Some of the guys thought we should put all our efforts into the hayloft before we tried to raise any money, but when I told them how much I already had to shell out, they were a little more understanding.

Cory was the most ornery. "We'll get blown out in that first tournament. We won't have had any time for practicing. I want to be the center. Dallas, can I be the center?"

"If you don't start working as hard as the rest of us, you won't even be starting."

He looked shocked. The truth was, I hadn't figured on Cory starting anyway. I knew Jimmy could shoot, even though he wasn't very good on defense. And we knew each other well enough to know where the other would be on the court all the time. So, in spite of his lack of speed, I thought

Jimmy would probably be the other forward besides me. Toby would have to be center because, though he wasn't the biggest by much, he was the heaviest, and he would be harder to push around.

The guards would be chosen from the other four: Bugsy, Ryan, Cory, and Brent. Cory the redhead was a little bigger than the other three, who—except for their coloring—could have been triplets in size and speed. I would just have to see who could dribble and pass the best.

I would also have to know who could play the best defense. Because if we were going to be the smallest team in a league of teams that already had the advantage of experience over us, we were going to have to shine on defense to even have a chance.

Ooh, boy, were we tired every night! Except for Cory, who seemed to find the easiest jobs on each assignment, it seemed that everyone was working hard. Sometimes we'd get jobs that took just one or two guys, like raking someone's leaves. Then we might get a job that took all of us, like clearing the hayloft.

That was a two-night job. Mrs. Ferguson said we could just drop all the hay out the window and down into the old corral that hadn't seen any livestock for years. It wasn't easy, crawling up into that loft with old hay baling hooks, a step ladder, and a tape measure.

Our first bit of good news came the first night when we cleared away enough of the haymow to make room for the stepladder. Jimmy and I measured from the rim to the foor. Whoever had put that hoop up there in the first place was a true basketball fan. It was exactly ten feet.

There was no backboard. The rim was just screwed directly to the wall, so if you drove up to it for a layup, you bounced off the wall just after releasing the ball.

Some of the guys wanted to start shooting right away, but we made them keep working. Finally, the day came that we were able to work to earn money and then spend the rest of the evening before bedtime in the loft, practicing.

We only had two basketballs, Jimmy's and mine. Mine

was rubber and had one spot where the inner bladder had been over-inflated and stuck out like a little bubble. That didn't cause any trouble unless you were unlucky enough to dribble right on that bubble.

Then the ball would bound away from you as if you had dribbled it off your foot, and every time it would bounce right to your defender. Jimmy's ball was nice, but it was hard and heavy. We figured it was the closest we'd come to the type of ball the Boys Amateur Basketball League would use, so we used his for more formal practicing.

We made a couple of hundred dollars the first week, and the guys were still pretty excited. But as time went on, it was a lot more fun to practice than to work. They were all curious about the starting lineup, but I didn't want to encourage or discourage anyone too much, so I said nothing.

Finally, we got the break we had been looking for. Mr. Calabresi told his company about us and what we were doing. His boss told Mr. Calabresi that if we would clear all the concrete out of an area behind their plant that had been used as a dumping ground for years, he would give us $25 dollars each.

It would take a whole Saturday and would cost us valuable practice time, but we couldn't pass up a total of $175. Better than that, the news of the job we did—it was terribly hard work—got back to the other workers in Mr. Calabresi's office, and people began hiring us for lots of odd jobs.

They figured that if a bunch of kids could lift heavy blocks of concrete and lug them to wheel barrows and push them to a spot where a front end loader could pick them up, we could certainly handle small jobs around their homes.

Some of them we had to turn down because we had no transportation, but the ones we did take earned us a lot more money. With a week to go before the delivery of the uniforms, we knew we were going to make it. We'd still have to take jobs, all of us, but the goal was in sight, and we could start concentrating on our game.

I didn't know much about the fine points of basketball, but I knew enough of the basics that we were working on dribbling, passing, shooting, free throws, rebounding, defense, and a little strategy.

The loft was miserable. In the late afternoons it was stifling, but with the door open the sun blinded us. With it shut, the big bulb we put in the ceiling provided just barely enough light to see the dark old hoop on the wall.

With only seven players, it was hard to set up game situations, but we did the best we could. I had everyone spending a lot of time on dribbling while running as fast as they could, and we all shot as much as possible from various spots on the floor.

Bugsy and Ryan turned out to be natural shooters and ball handlers. I was impressed with Cory's aggressiveness, which shouldn't have been a surprise. Brent was just too small to be very effective, but he was a hard worker and loved the game. We were going to have a good team.

Jimmy was a good shooter but slow and almost useless on defense. I wasn't getting in as much shooting as I really needed, so I found myself practicing at home when I got the chance. It helped, but it was tricky working out at two different basket heights every day.

Before we knew it, we were really looking forward to playing on a real court that had a hoop with a net, proper lighting, a good ball, and—most of all—competition.

One thing I stressed more than anything else on offense was free throw shooting. When we first started, even our best shooter, Jimmy, was making only about forty-five out of a hundred. I thought we should all be around 75 percent and made a rule that you couldn't do anything else in practice until you'd made ten free throws in a row.

The problem was, that kept the free throw line and one basketball tied up for quite a while, and the other ball would always seem to make the free throw shooter miss.

It was fun to find someone in the loft shooting whenever we arrived. We left both balls there as often as possible so anyone who was free could come and work out. We studied books from the library about strategy, playing defense against bigger opponents, stalling, and all the fundamentals.

The ball sounded strange banging off the plywood floor of that hayloft, and it never bounced true, the way it would off a hard court in a real gym. And it was so dark at our feet that we squinted to see the ball.

The old rim had a lot of give to it, and there was a trick to getting a bank shot in. The wall boards were so weird that if you shot straight, the ball always shot back past the front edge of the rim and would hardly ever drop through. The only way to make a bank shot was to shoot softly from the side.

I wasn't too sure what that would do to our game. What if the bounce off the real backboards at Jefferson High was totally different? Of course it would be. We tried to make swishes whenever we could, but with no net to slow the ball as it went through and very little light to see what was happening, we sometimes wondered whether we had scored or not.

The day our uniforms arrived, my parents let us have a little celebration at my house. We all giggled and teased each other as we came bounding out of the bedrooms and bathrooms in our new shorts and shirts. They looked great.

Just like with the baseball uniforms, I had number four. Toby was forty-four, Jimmy forty, Bugsy one, Ryan two, Brent thirty-three, and Cory thirty-four. All the uniforms fit nicely, and I made the rule that we would never wear them in practice. Everyone wanted to, including me, but there was no way we wanted to smell like an old barn the first time we lined up in that B.A.B.L. tournament.

While the guys were putting away their uniforms, I talked privately with Brent and then Cory. "I want you to know that I'm not going to be putting you in the starting lineup. You'll get to play a lot, and you'll be important to the team. Maybe after the tournament I'll change my mind and start you, but for now my starters will be Toby at center, Jimmy and me at forwards, and Bugsy and Ryan at guards."

Brent took it real well. It wasn't a surprise to him at all. He even wanted me to know that he wouldn't feel bad if he didn't play at all during some games. "But that won't happen, Brent. We're going to need you to play probably about a total of at least a quarter."

"Really?"

"Really! We've got such a few players that we're going to get tired. I may have to move to center to give Toby a rest, then Bugsy or Ryan will have to fill in at center, and you'll have to come in at guard. I'm not just trying to be nice, Brent. You really are going to be needed on this team."

Cory, however, didn't take the news so well.

4
Intimidation

C ory stayed at my house long after everyone else had left, arguing about my decision that he would not be a starter on the Baker Street Sports Club basketball team.

He cried, he raised his voice, he pleaded. But I had to hold firm. "Being the captain is not easy. I have to make tough decisions. I'm telling you, Cory, you're going to get plenty of chances to play. In fact, like I told Brent, I'm going to need you to play a total of a least a quarter of each game."

Cory wasn't convinced, but at least he didn't quit. I think he liked his uniform so much that he didn't even want to think about giving that up. "I want to prove to you that I should start. Every time I get the ball, I'm gonna be shooting and scoring so you'll have to start me."

I told him he played good defense. "But I don't think you're a good enough shooter that you should try to shoot every time."

"I'm going to!"

"And if you do, I'll have to pull you and put someone else in."

"Who? Brent? He can't be your only substitute!"

I spoke more quietly to try to calm him down. "You'd better change your attitude, Cory. I could not only keep you on the bench, but I could also kick you off the team, even out of the club."

Mr. Lemke called me on Friday night that week, but I was with the guys in the hayloft, nervously practicing for the last time. When I got home, my dad told me to call him.

"Yeah, Dallas, I just wanted you to know that the gym will be open at eight tomorrow morning, so you and your team can practice as early as you want."

"Really? In the gym?"

"Sure. All the teams will be there, and three courts will be open. The first game isn't until noon, so you can shoot in your sweats until the pairings have been announced."

"Sweats?"

"Right. Your sweat suits."

"Uh, we don't have any."

"Well, then you can practice in your street clothes, as long as you use the proper shoes. You won't want to practice in your uniforms, because you may not be playing until much later in the day."

I felt sick. That would be awful, being the new team and having to practice in street clothes while all the other teams glided around in warm-ups. "When do they announce the pairings?"

Mr. Lemke hesitated. "Uh, let's see, eleven o'clock. Then we start the first game at noon and play one every two hours until the first round is over. The winners play Monday night with games at five and seven. The championship is Tuesday night at six."

I told Mr. Lemke not to be concerned if we didn't show up until eleven Saturday morning. He sounded puzzled and worried, but I promised him we would be there. "You'll point us to the locker room at the right time?"

He assured me he would, the sound of concern still in his voice. I wasn't going to let my team feel weird by being the only ones there practicing in street clothes, especially when we were the new team as it was. The next morning, we were in the hayloft as usual.

Cory was quiet, which was unusual. Very unusual. On defense, he was a maniac, fouling every time someone else had the ball. I told him I liked his aggressiveness, but that he should be careful not to hurt anyone before the game.

The loft was cold that morning, and we worked on positioning—where everyone would stand on offense and defense. We decided on a zone defense instead of man-to-man because the teams we would face would be bigger and more experienced. Any one of us could be beaten on any play by a better player, so we had to help each other out.

Jimmy's dad and mine dropped us off at Jefferson High at about ten-thirty that morning. We told them we'd call them as soon as we found out when our game was so they could call the other parents, and those who wanted to could come.

It was scary to walk into that big school, just the seven of us. We had our little canvas bags, all except Ryan who arrived with his new uniform and shoes in a brown paper bag. The other teams were already there with their brothers and sisters and parents and friends, milling around, running up and down the halls, and shooting baskets in all the gyms.

At the registration table I found Mr. Lemke, who didn't look at all like he sounded on the telephone. I had pictured him as a tall, distinguished looking man with gray hair. Actually he was kind of squatty with thinning, almost gone black hair and thick glasses. But he was just as nice in person as he had been all along on the phone.

He showed us where the locker rooms were, and we went in and stored our uniforms. The other players looked at us curiously, but none of them greeted us or asked us anything. They had to know there was a new team in the league, and they had to be wondering what we looked like or where we were from, but either they didn't recognize us as the new entry or they didn't care.

I found that hard to believe. The Baker Street Sports Club had earned a good reputation in the local papers for our baseball games. These guys had to be at least a little worried that we might be good in basketball too.

We sat in the bleachers by ourselves, but I was shocked at how many people were in the stands. There had to be about a thousand people. I had expected a couple of hundred at the most, figuring that just one set of parents and maybe a brother or sister of each player would show up.

It was clear that this was an unusual league. Every other team seemed to have at least two coaches and a trainer. Guys were getting their ankles taped before they put their shoes on. Some of the teams had color coordinated duffle bags and warm-up suits. And they all had a bunch of new basketballs. We hadn't brought either of ours, hoping we could borrow a few from the league for pre-game practice.

Finally the big moment came. Mr. Lemke had one of the little sisters, who had been named B.A.B.L. queen for the year, pick the teams from a hat. He made the announcement of the pairings over the loud speaker.

"In the first game at noon today, the visiting team will be—the Beavers!"

All the Beavers and their fans jumped and screamed, and then I saw something that left me speechless. The Beavers had cheerleaders too! No wonder there was such a big crowd! These teams all had cheerleaders—all but us, of course—and *their* parents and friends came to the games too!

"Their opponents, the home team in the first game—the undefeated, defending champion Condors!"

You could hardly hear the name of the team. The place went crazy, and the noise was deafening as soon as he had said "undefeated, defending . . . " Everyone knew the Condors, and everyone was buzzing about their new secret weapon this year, the giant center.

A kid in front of us whispered to his friend. "They say he's almost seven feet tall and about twenty years old. Nobody knows how he got in this league. Somebody said he threatened Mr. Lemke when he showed his birth certificate and made him let him play. Two of his teammates have been knocked out cold running into him under the basket. He can slam dunk, and he even punched out one of his own coaches!"

It sounded like a bunch of phony rumors to me, but I

didn't know. I admit I was looking for the big kid just as much as anyone else was. There was a big guy sitting with the Condors up in the balcony, but he looked like he was in college. And he *did* look about twice the size of the other Condors. That couldn't have been him. Could it?

The two o'clock game would be the Falcons against the Hippos. At four, the Grenadiers would take on the Eagles. That left us to play the Dolphins in the last game at six o'clock. Jimmy went to call his dad, so his dad could tell my dad and spread the word.

I told the guys I thought it was great that we were in the last game. Cory wasn't so sure. "Why? I'm ready now."

I tried to explain. "None of us are ready yet. We have to see these teams, how they play, who they've got, how this league works. Let's scout each team and try to remember what they do in case we play them in a later round."

"What if we don't make it to the next round, Dal?"

"Then we can be ready for when we play them during the season. While we watch each game, I'll tell you who you would be guarding on each team and how I think we can handle them."

The guys gathered around closer as the Condors and the Beavers ran out onto the floor. But none of us said anything. We were shocked. In fact, we were ready to pack it in right then. There was no way in the world we could compete in this league. How could we?

I mean, those two teams were just warming up. They still had their sweats on, and their cheerleaders were trying to get the crowd excited. But they looked like high school kids. They floated around the court. Their passes were crisp, their drills were flawless.

Each of the fifteen boys on each side knew how to dribble and pass and shoot, and they had that air about them as if they had been born to play basketball. Suddenly it dawned on me. This was no ordinary park district league for kids who couldn't make the teams at their schools.

This was the real thing. This was a league for families who had kids who were too good for their school teams. This was

31

for players who were going to be high school and college and maybe even pro stars some day.

Their parents were wealthy enough to afford not only the registration fees and the equipment but also to have paid coaches and all the extras. They had water cans, first aid kits, towels, little chalk boards for the coaches, everything.

Maybe they just looked good from this angle because they were only practicing, but somehow I knew we were in over our heads. At least we had been wrong about the Condors secret weapon. There wasn't anyone on the court over five-ten, though the Condors had only fourteen players, while the Beavers had the maximum fifteen.

Just before the referee whistled them off the floor for the introductions, we were proved wrong again. Out onto the court jogged the giant we had heard about. And he looked mean.

The Condors had a fancy drill where they lined up on either side of the basket and alternated shooting layups and rebounding for each other. That was over, and the teams were just idly shooting from all over the court—and making most everything.

The giant loped around the half court to loosen up, then eased under the basket where a pass always seemed to be waiting for him. He gathered in the ball slowly and nonchalantly, though not awkwardly, and turned to stuff it through.

He did that three times, then walked to the bench and sat waiting to be introduced. If he wasn't seven feet tall, he sure looked it. And if he was twelve, I was the Easter bunny.

5

Scouting the Giant Condor

I could see from the looks on the faces of my teammates that we were all thinking the same thing. We could not compete in this league, and we should have checked into it more carefully before spending all our money on the uniforms and registration.

For sure, we wouldn't want our friends and families to see us humiliated in the first round of the tournament. That's why we all scowled at Jimmy when he returned, beaming. "Everybody's going to be here at six! We have to win!"

The opening tip off of the first game was the only good thing that happened to the Beavers the whole time. We had discovered that the giant Condor's name was Jack Bastable and that his coach's name was Petey Maxwell. Right, Petey. That's what everybody called him. Because even though he had a pair of eleven-year-old twin sons—Mickey and Michael, who played guard for him—he didn't look much older than they did.

These were the two kids the local junior high coach had been drooling over for years, ever since they had made names for themselves in peewee basketball. But there was no way they would play school ball, now that they were in the B.A.B.L. and were being given careful supervision by their own father. He was known to have been a starting guard at a Big Ten school fifteen years before.

The Beaver center was clearly not going to compete against the nearly seven-foot Bastable, if that's what he really was. So his coach had apparently told him not to try. He crouched in the circle as if he were going to give it everything he had, but when the ref tossed the ball up, the Beaver center skipped away from the circle and intercepted the tip as the big man banged it toward his teammates.

The play worked perfectly. The Beaver center picked off the ball and flung it over his shoulder to a teammate, a small guard with quick feet, and he beat the Condors to the bucket for an easy lay-up. The crowd was stunned, assuming the Condors would dominate the little Beavers, but suddenly it was 2-0, and the Condors looked befuddled.

But only temporarily. While one of the Maxwell twins took the ball out and passed it in to his brother, big Bastable loped down the court and planted himself near the basket, just outside the lane. Mike passed to Mickey, who appeared to be driving toward the hoop, drawing the defense away from the big man.

He then arched a high, looping pass toward the backboard, where Jack, with perfect timing, leaped and slammed the ball home. You could see the air leave the Beavers. They were already beat, and they knew it. How were they going to stop this guy?

But in truth, Jack Bastable was only part of their trouble. The Condors immediately set up in a full court press defense, covering all the Beavers man to man. They tried to pass the ball in, but one of the Maxwell brothers stole it, passed to his brother, alley-ooped to Bastable, and it was 4-2.

When the same thing happened on the next two inbound passes and the Beavers found themselves down 8-2, their coach called a time-out. I told my teammates what I thought he would be planning.

"They have to do something about everything. They need to beat the press, keep the big man away from the boards, and try to slow down the guards."

I was right, even though they were not successful. The

Beavers came up with a plan that allowed them to at least get the ball in play, but when their forward missed a shot, Bastable was there to swipe it out of the air and fire a lead pass to the Maxwells on the fast break.

But the Beavers were ready for that too. They raced down the court and set up an unusual defense. They put three men on Bastable, surrounding him at the baseline. Their guards tried to stay with the Maxwell twins and were doing a fairly good job.

One of the twins tried another alley-oop to Bastable, but with three men on him his timing was off, and he missed the pass. It bounded back to Mike Maxwell, who fired to one of his forwards in the corner—who, of course, had no one guarding him.

Swisheroo. Incredible. The triple teaming of Bastable did the Beavers no good. They couldn't shoot without his blocking their shots to the Maxwells, who fed the uncovered forwards for baseline shots from both sides of the court. At the end of the first quarter, the Condors led 20-2 and were starting to use their substitutes freely.

The Baker Street Sports Club was somber. No one was saying much. Except Cory, of course. "So, what's the strategy, coach? Who are we going to guard? Maybe you want all seven of us on the court, three on the giant Condor and the rest on the other members of the team."

I had to admit it didn't look as if we would face the Condors. We would have to win the first round and the semifinal to face them for the championship, but I didn't see how we could compete. "Let's concentrate on the Beavers. We'll be facing them during the regular season."

Jimmy shook his head. "Don't kid yourself. They have pretty good players too. Unless we have a big man like the Condors, even the Beavers will eat us alive. I was talkin' to a guy at the scorers' table on my way back from makin' the phone call, and he told me he thought this would be a pretty good game. You wanna know why? Because it was the Beavers the Condors beat for the league championship last year. They beat 'em in overtime by two points."

"You're kidding."

"That's what he said. Of course, the Condors didn't have Bastable then. But they had the Maxwell twins and those two pretty-shooting forwards. They're tough. In the regular season last year they lost only to the Condors."

We all looked at each other, wondering if we shouldn't just sneak into the locker room, get our stuff, and slither away, never to be heard from again. I hate to admit it, but if enough of the guys had said anything close to that, I would have done it. It's not like me. I'm not a quitter or a chicken. I don't run from a tough game. But this was ridiculous. If the rest of the teams in this league were this good, what were we doing there?

Mr. Maxwell, the Condor coach, showed a little class when he played mostly reserves for the rest of the game and won 60-25. I heard people talking about how much of a hot dog and hothead he could be when things weren't going his way, but everything was perfect for him in the Beaver game, so we didn't get to see the other side of him.

The Falcon-Hippo game was much less interesting. It was a low-scoring contest, and neither team looked particularly sharp in its shooting. However, both teams were wonderful at the fundamentals and didn't make any mistakes or cause a lot of turnovers.

We watched that game with a little less interest, because we knew that unless something drastic happened to the Condors, they would sweep away the winner with little effort and breeze into the finals.

The Hippos won by five, but basically we felt sorry for them. At five o'clock on Monday, they would have to face the Condors. We wondered if they would carry clubs or just give up!

The four o'clock game that afternoon was the one we watched carefully. At least I told the guys to watch it that way. It wasn't that we really thought we would win our game and face the winner of this one at seven on Monday, but if we somehow managed to pull off a miracle, that's what would happen.

The Grenadiers were playing the Eagles, and I paid less attention than I should have because I was sure we would lose in the first round. It was a terrible attitude, but I didn't know what else to think. By now, even Cory was quiet, and I wanted to know why. Maybe now was a good time to make up with him. I needed him to be a good member of the team, even if he was going to sit on the bench most of the time.

With so few players on our team, we would probably get laughed at, and it was going to be crucial that we all had a team spirit. I moved down one row and left a couple of seats until I was sitting right next to him. "What do you think, Red?"

He wasn't amused. "Don't call me Red. My mother calls me Red, and I hate it."

"Sorry, Cory. I was just wondering what you were thinking by now."

"You mean about not starting?"

I nodded. "Or about our playing in this league at all."

"I wondered if you would ever ask. Dallas, I don't think we want to embarrass ourselves out there in front of all those people. At least I know I don't. If we're going to play, I guess I'm glad I won't be starting."

"But if we play at all, Cory, you'll have to help. And I need you to want to."

"I don't want to, and it's not because I'm not starting. I don't think any of us want to. Except you maybe. If you think any of the others agree with you, you'd better ask them."

The trouble was, I wasn't sure I'd disagree with them. Maybe it was better to drop out now and let the Dolphins advance by forfeit than to play the winner of the Grenadier/ Eagle game. Anyway, I had to ask the guys.

6

Meeting the Giant

I couldn't have been more shocked. I started asking the other guys what they thought, and they were disappointed in me that I was ready to give up. They all had basically the same idea. "We know we'll probably lose, but what about Nehemiah and Gideon? They probably thought they'd lose too, but they didn't. You're the boss, Dallas. You decide. If you quit, we quit. If you play, we play."

I had to take a walk. The Grenadiers were manhandling the Eagles. They looked a lot like our team, with no real big players, a couple of thick, slow ones, and some good speed and shooting. They were excellent on defense.

As I stepped down from the bleachers and walked down the aisle to the corridor where I could be alone, I made mental notes of who would be guarding whom and what they might have to watch for. That made me wonder if I hadn't already made up my mind to stay and play. I guess I had, but I needed to pray about this one.

All through the halls there were parents and fans and players from the teams that had already played. I looked for a lonely spot where I wouldn't be noticed. I wanted to sit down and pretend like I was napping so I could pray. It wasn't that I was ashamed of it, but I knew I wasn't supposed to make it real obvious to people. That would be like showing off and pretending you were real spiritual or something.

As I passed the main entrance, I saw Jack Bastable with what appeared to be a sister and his parents. They were talking to him as if he were a child. "You played a good game, Jack. Really good. We were so proud of you. You scored lots of points!"

He was smiling real big, and I realized I had not really seen him smile on the court. I thought maybe I had been too far away, but I knew that if he had smiled, I'd have noticed. I nearly bumped into him.

I was surprised that he wasn't as huge as everyone had said. I guessed him at six foot three or maybe four at the most. There was no doubt he could stuff a basketball, and he was a good head taller than anyone else in the league. But he was no seven-footer, and he certainly didn't seem mean.

I knew all the stories about his beating people up were just rumors. I reached out a hand to him. "You played well."

He looked sheepishly down at me as he wrapped his huge paw around my little hand. "Thank you."

The sound was strange, as if it came from deep in his throat, maybe even as if it were a different language. I wanted to hear more, to figure this guy out. "Congratulations on the win. You been playing long?"

He stopped and stared at me, as if thinking. "Almost all my life." He hadn't started to grow whiskers yet.

The voice was the same. He was working hard to speak clearly. His family was smiling at him. I had to keep the conversation going. "You're a big guy. It's hard to believe you're just twelve."

He smiled again and held out his wrist for me to see. He had a plastic digital watch with an alarm and a stopwatch built in. "Birthday last week. Got this."

"It's nice." His parents smiled at me and led him out. Then it dawned on me. Jack Bastable was retarded. He was indeed just twelve, even though he was huge and looked older. How he had learned to control his body and play such graceful basketball was beyond me, but maybe because it was the one thing he concentrated most on, it made him that much better.

He had been scary on the court. The Beavers had guarded him cautiously. He looked determined and, yes, mean at times. A few guys bounced off him and hit the floor while competing with him for rebounds, but he hadn't come close to fighting or even arguing or raising his voice.

He had not smiled, but that was probably because it took so much concentration for him to just play the game at the level he did. I debated with myself about whether to tell the other guys what I had learned. Maybe I would save it until when we played the Condors in the regular season. I knew well that it was unlikely we'd face them in this pre-season tournament, but I also knew that we were going to stay in the league.

I hadn't prayed about it yet. I was still going to, but running into Jack Bastable and his family had been like an answer to a prayer that hadn't even been prayed yet. I knew that if he could overcome a handicap like that, surely we could play in a league where everyone looked better than we did.

I found an empty hallway and hurried down to the far end. I sat on the floor, my back against the wall. I drew up my knees and buried my face in them. I thanked God for letting me find out the truth about Jack Bastable. I asked for the strength and the knowledge I would need to be the captain of the smallest, least experienced, and least likely to win team in the whole league.

And then I asked Him for help in dealing with Cory. I knew he was the key to our team because he was the one whose attitude could make us or break us. As usual, I prayed for Jimmy, because he had heard so many of the Bible stories and devotionals I had read, and he was close to coming to church with me.

My head was still down when I heard someone coming. I thought it might be a janitor who would tell me to move along. I wanted to appear as if I was just sleeping, so I jumped when a hand touched my shoulder.

"What're you doin', O'Neil?" It was Cory.

"Resting. Thinking." It was true but not the whole truth, of course, and that made me feel guilty.

"You're doin' more than that, aren't you?"

"What do you mean?"

"You're prayin'!"

"What makes you think that?"

"Well, are ya, or aren't ya?"

"I am, but so what? How did you know?"

Cory slid down beside me. "Jimmy said he figured that's what you were off doin'. I had to see for myself."

"Satisfied?"

"I guess. You're a little weird, ya know?"

"I s'pose, Cory. I've thought the same about you."

"So, what were you prayin' about?"

"It's personal."

"Well, I should hope so, Dal! Were you prayin' for me?"

"A little."

"Like what?"

"I told you. It's personal."

"Yeah! I'm personal to me too! You want God to strike me dead, take me to heaven, what?"

"Nothing like striking you dead, Cory. Where'd you get that idea?"

"My aunt. She's always tellin' me that if I don't straighten up, God's gonna strike me dead and send me to hell."

I was praying silently. "That's not the kind of God I'd want to pray to, Cory. Would you?"

"No! So why are you?"

"I'm not. I don't want to put down your aunt, but I don't believe that's what God is like. Do you?"

Cory shrugged.

I prayed that God would give me the right words. "The God I pray to loves me. Loves everybody. Doesn't want anybody to die and go to hell. In fact, He's made it easy for us to know Him and be sure we're not going to hell."

Cory was nervous. I didn't want to bother him or pressure him. Maybe I had said enough for the first time.

"Is that what you were praying about, Dallas?"

"Actually, no. I was praying that you would have a good attitude and help the team."

He looked at me. "Yeah?"

I nodded.

"And what if I don't change my attitude? That mean you were just prayin' to the ceiling?"

"Not necessarily. I don't know. What do you think?"

"I think I'm gonna have a better attitude, but I don't know if that means God answered your prayer or not. I just came down here to tell you that the Grenadiers beat the Eagles by twelve, and we're on in half an hour."

Suddenly I was nervous. It was too late to back out, even if I had wanted to. The guys figured I was being brave because of the Bible stories I had told, and even though I didn't feel brave, I was going to have to act that way.

We jogged toward the locker room. When we were out of earshot of anyone else, Cory called over his shoulder. "Do me a favor, O'Neil. Keep prayin' for me."

"Don't worry. And if you have a good game and don't get into any trouble, I'll let you come to church with me tomorrow and you can hear some more stories."

"And learn to pray? No thanks."

I ignored him.

While we were dressing we noticed the Dolphins at the other end of the locker room. Their coach came over. "Where's *your* coach, son?"

I shook his hand. "We don't have one. I'm the captain. Dallas O'Neil."

He introduced himself as Cliff Flesher and told me a little about his team. They had finished last in the league the last two years in a row. "We won one two years ago and two last year, so we're hoping to win at least four this year. Of course, we're glad you boys joined the league so maybe you can take over the cellar for a while."

I smiled as he walked away. Some of the guys wanted to know what he meant. I told them what I thought. "He thinks we're automatically going to go winless and be in last place, so that even if his team only wins four games again, they'll finish no worse than second to last. How do we feel about that?"

I didn't expect a lot of noise. I just expected the kinds of looks I got from the Baker Street Sports Club. They were fierce and determined. As for me, I was just eager to run out onto a real basketball court and dribble and shoot a little.

Mr. Lemke sent someone in to tell us where our bench was and which end of the court we could warm up on. "Head out any time you're ready."

We didn't have any set drills because there were so few of us. I found three good basketballs and told the guys to just run out and start shooting and rebounding for each other. "If anyone says anything or laughs because there's only seven of us, just ignore them and get more determined to show them how good we are. Ready?"

They all said they were, but every face looked just as scared as my own. By then I didn't care if we won or not. I just didn't want us to embarrass ourselves.

As we ran out, everyone stopped right at the entrance to the gym and sort of bumped into each other, insisting they didn't want to be first. They looked to me. Good grief. "Oh, OK, I'll be first, but stay close behind."

As I went from the dark hallway that led from the locker rooms into the light in the gym, I squinted and looked for our end of the court. There it was, gleaming and bright. I dribbled the length of the court, feeling conspicuous but also great because of being on such a nice, hard floor.

I started feeling more and more confident, and I heard the announcer talking to the crowd. "Welcome the newest entry into the league, the Baker Street Sports Club!"

People clapped politely, and I'm sure the rest of the guys felt as embarrassed as I did. I picked up speed and drove toward the basket. One more bounce, and I would guide the ball toward a lay-up with my right hand.

But the ball bounced off my foot, and I chased it all the way to the wall under the basket to the laughter of the crowd.

7
Playing the Dolphins

I should have left well enough alone. Trying to salvage something from my goof, I flung myself toward the ball and batted it back toward my teammates, as if I was saving a loose ball from going out of bounds.

They weren't watching, so the ball hurtled at them like a line drive and knocked another ball out of their hands and hit two as they went for a rebound. I felt so stupid I could have dug a hole and crawled in.

But when I looked around, my face red, no one was paying much attention. Those who were watching us rather than the Dolphins were probably just wondering where the rest of our team was.

We shot around a while, and I noticed that the other guys were having the same trouble I was. It was so exciting, so exhilarating playing on a real court that we were running and jumping and shooting and sweating and really getting into it.

I called all the guys around. "We'd better cool down a little. This is great, isn't it?" They smiled and nodded, eager to keep practicing. "We can't get all worn out before the game, guys. Let's line up and shoot ten free throws each and then sit down.

Brent and I stood under the basket while the others took turns shooting their free throws. If the ball missed to the left or dropped through the net, Brent fired it back to the shooter. If it missed right, I tossed it back.

Hardly anyone could hit more than one or two free throws out of ten, we were all so nervous. Cory hit seven though, and he kept smiling at me. I pretended not to notice. I couldn't change the lineup now, despite his change of attitude and his good—or lucky—shooting.

The whistle blew, and the horn sounded. The ref told me to have the starters check in with the scorekeeper. I wasn't even sure what he meant until I saw the Dolphins line up at the scorer's table and announce themselves to the man with the book.

We had only a second to chat before we were to get out on the court, so I simply told them to watch me, stay cool, and not rush. "We're playing a zone, so don't worry about which man to guard. You take anyone who comes into your area." I pointed to the other end of the court. "Remember, if they get the tip, race down there and get into position as fast as you can."

Toby would play a high post, or out near the top of the key past the free throw line. Bugsy and Ryan would position themselves on either side of the free throw line, and Jimmy and I would play under the basket, collapsing in on their center and forwards as necessary. If we couldn't handle them, we'd bring Toby back in for a low post.

Their center was a couple of inches taller than Toby, but I didn't want to just give up on the tip the way the Beavers did against Jack Bastable. It worked for them, but I figured that was mostly luck. I mean, they scored the first bucket, but it was the only one they made in the whole first quarter.

The tip went to the Dolphins, and we ran to get into position. It was a good thing their first shot missed, because none of us tried to defend against it. We were all so careful to get to the right spots on the floor that we all but ignored the other team and the ball.

They passed it back and forth a couple of times and one of their guards sent up an air ball that would have fallen right into my hands if I'd been ready. It flew out of bounds, and suddenly it was our ball.

I had instructed that Ryan was to take the ball out each time and toss it to Bugsy, who would bring it up the court. But in the excitement, I just jumped out of bounds for the ball. The ref gave it to me, but here came Ryan, and I realized what I had done. He was on his way out of bounds to get the ball from me when I tossed it to him. He caught it and stepped out, and that made it Dolphins' ball.

I slapped myself on the forehead and shouted an apology to my teammates. Just when we should have been getting loosened up, I, the captain, was playing like a maniac. It was making everybody crazy. As soon as the Dolphins inbounded the ball, Toby wrapped his arms around their center for a foul.

By the time we got to our own end of the court with the ball, we were trailing by two. Bugsy made the mistake of falling for one of the oldest tricks in the book. The defense appeared to leave the middle open, so he tried to pass right through the lane to me.

I looked wide open, but as soon as he let fly the pass, they sagged back in and batted the ball to one of their fast-breaking guards and scored easily. We continued to make those kinds of mistakes for the next several minutes, and our first two shots weren't even close.

Suddenly we were down 10-0 to last year's worst team in the league, and we were starting to holler at each other. The Dolphins were enjoying themselves immensely, grinning from ear to ear and doing everything but laugh at us. I called a time out.

With two minutes to talk, I spent the first thirty seconds just looking into the eyes of my players. Toby looked down, but everyone else was still fresh and eager. I asked Toby if he needed a break, if he wanted Cory to go in for him.

"No way!"

"Then listen up, everybody. We can beat this team. Sure they're up by ten, and we aren't on the board yet, but they've missed a lot of shots. Let's put more pressure on but be careful not to foul. Let's not give them any freebies. Our shots will come, and they'll start to drop, so let's not give up. Don't try to make them back all at once. Let's see if we can close the gap to six by the end of the quarter."

We did better than that. I whispered to Bugsy to bring the ball up as usual, fake a pass through the lane, and shoot. "We need a quick bucket." It worked perfectly. He had been passing every time down the floor, but this time he faked, got the defense off balance, and hit a fifteen-foot jumper.

We clapped and high-fived each other, and Bugsy was so psyched up he stole the ball and scored on a fast break. We had closed the gap to six within thirty seconds of taking the floor again.

They missed, got their own rebound, and missed again, this time the ball coming down to Toby. He hit me at mid-court, and I drove toward the basket. I heard footsteps close enough behind me to block the shot, and I saw Jimmy out of the corner of my eye.

He was moving, none too fast, a little behind me to my right. We had practiced this play in my driveway for years. No one was worried about the slow kid following the play, so without looking, I passed it to him over my shoulder.

My defender went up with me as I flew toward the basket. Jimmy took the pass, pulled up, and hit a long set shot. If it had missed, I would have been able to put in the rebound because I sailed past the basket just as the ball dropped through.

We were within four and getting excited when the buzzer sounded, signaling the end of the first quarter.

In the second quarter I took my first shot from the corner. It felt so good when it dropped through, popping the net without brushing the rim, that I felt hot. I made four more in that quarter alone to lead our team at the half with ten points.

But the Dolphins had played us even in the quarter and still led by four.

In the locker room I announced the substitutions for the

third quarter. "Brent for Bugsy. Ryan, you bring the ball up. Cory for Jimmy."

Jimmy winced. I told him he needed a break. "We need your good shooting for the fourth quarter."

"You mean I'm not gonna play in the third quarter at all?"

"Yes, you are. But we need to save your strength."

Cory made the difference in the third quarter. He sank two of five shots, three of four free throws, dove after loose balls, tied up the Dolphins for two jump balls, stole the ball twice, and was all over the court. He even blocked a shot, timing his leap perfectly to drill a shot by their center right back into his face.

He inspired us—there's no other way to say it. We led by two going into the final period, and there was no stopping us. I pointed out a weakness before we started the fourth quarter. "They're dead tired. I know we're tired too, but we've been working so hard and under such bad conditions, this is like playing in heaven.

"Don't get overconfident. Play steady till the end. We can outlast them. They have to use more subs, and we're still in better shape."

Jimmy scored eight in the last period. I added six. Bugsy had four. We won by six and got a nice round of applause. We left the court thinking we were the best team in that league. Bring on the Grenadiers, and then bring on the Condors. Bring on Jack Bastable.

We didn't care. We could have whipped the Los Angeles Lakers right then.

8
Cory the Great

In the locker room we were all whooping and hollering, and Cory was in the middle of it. "Only played a quarter, but scored seven points! Was I somethin', huh?"

He was only teasing, and we all laughed. When the other guys were in the shower, Cory sat down next to me in front of my locker. "What was that you said about helpin' the team and not gettin' into any trouble?"

I looked over at him. "I don't remember. What *did* I say?"

"You said you'd let me come to church with you."

I was stunned. "You really want to? I mean, yeah, sure you can come. But, uh, are you serious?"

"Why not? Let's just say I wanna hear more stories, like you said."

I told him we'd pick him up at nine-thirty. "And you did help the team, Cory. Really. You turned the game around." He smiled and nodded, his red hair wet and matted.

Most of our parents were waiting to give us rides home. They were pretty proud. I got the feeling that most of the mothers weren't quite sure what had gone on, and most of the fathers could hardly believe we'd come back from being down by ten to win by six.

Jimmy and his parents rode home with my mom and dad, my two little sisters, and me. It was crowded in the station wagon. And strangely quiet. Jimmy usually talked a mile a minute, but he said hardly anything, except a couple of polite answers to my mother, who asked about school.

I thought maybe he was upset because I had benched him during most of the third quarter. But that strategy had paid off. I tried to make him feel better by talking loudly so everyone could hear.

"Boy, Jim, you really carried us in the fourth quarter. You made sure we stayed ahead with all that great shooting."

He nodded. "Yeah."

I tried again. "I thought Cory played good ball. He's a pretty good little substitute, but probably not ready to start. I mean, if I started him, it would have to be at one of the guard positions, maybe for Bugsy."

He spoke softly, as if wanting to end the conversation. "Bugsy played well."

"Yeah, but I may have to find a spot for Cory. He's aggressive, and a better shooter than I thought. Not so wild. He might get tired after a while, as hard as he plays, and I don't think he's going to be much of a ballhandler, but—"

Jimmy spoke just above a whisper. "But you're lookin' for a place for him, and I'm the most likely one for him to replace, right?"

I should have told him right away that he was wrong, that that wasn't what I was thinking at all. Because it wasn't. I just couldn't believe that's what was bothering him. That wasn't like Jimmy. I hesitated, but then I tried to make up for it.

"Not at all, Jim. There's nobody on the team that shoots that long set shot like you. We need you in the lineup for at least three periods a game, maybe three and a half, like tonight."

"Three and a quarter."

I was talking softly now too, so I wouldn't embarrass him. "Is that what's bothering you? You felt you didn't play enough tonight? I thought the strategy worked just right. You were rested up for the end of the third and all of the fourth period, and Cory did well while you were out."

Jimmy didn't argue. He just looked away. I said a few

more things, funny things, meaningless things, just to get a response. I got nothing. He was upset, and somehow I couldn't believe it had to do with the game. In fact, in the fourth quarter he had acted like his usual self to me and to everyone else.

It was still bothering me when I got home. I felt good like you always do after winning. Somehow the aches and pains and tiredness are worth it if the score comes out right. When we lost baseball games that summer, I was so dead tired and achey that I limped around, groaning all through the house.

But when we won, I lounged on the couch with a lemonade and knew it was worth all the effort. That night after beating the Dolphins, I sat munching popcorn with the family and idly listened to my dad talk about getting to bed early because of church in the morning.

"Cory wants to go with us, Dad. I told him we'd pick him up at nine-thirty."

"Cory? Really?"

I nodded. My parents knew how many times I had tried to get the guys to go with me. I felt good that we had a Sunday school and church that you didn't have to be embarrassed about if you brought somebody. The people were friendly. My teacher was a nice young guy. Our pastor knew how to talk to people even if they didn't come to church much.

Mom answered the phone. It was Jimmy. I hobbled to the kitchen. "What's happenin', Jim?"

"I just wanted to tell you what was botherin' me, that's all."

"Good. I'm glad you called. I mean, I knew it couldn't have been the game. You seemed happy during the game."

"Yeah, I was. It was after the game. On the way out to the car, Cory was braggin' that you invited him to go some-where with you tomorrow. Where you goin'? Aren't I still your best friend? Or are you replacin' me with Cory?"

I thought before I spoke. "Jimmy, you don't ever have to be jealous of anybody. You and I have been friends too long.

Anyway, you know where I go every Sunday, morning and night. Or did you forget?"

"I know where you're goin'. I was just wonderin' why you invited him and not me."

I hardly knew what to say. "Jimmy! How many times have I asked you? You *never* want to."

He was silent for a few seconds. "I didn't know Cory would go."

"I didn't either, Jim. I'm as surprised as you are."

"He said you asked him."

"Well, I sort of did. I told him if he played well and stayed out of trouble, I'd let him go with me. He had to remind me that I'd even said it."

Jimmy didn't say anything. I didn't know if he was waiting to be asked, or what. "Are you telling me that now that Cory is going, you want to come too?"

He was slow to answer. "You probably don't want me to. Your car will be crowded. Picking up two people will make you late. Anyway, I'd be butting in."

I smiled. He was making up all the excuses. I decided to just answer them one by one. "I want you to come. There's plenty of room in the car. We'll get started early, or you could ride your bike over here and go with us when we pick up Cory. And you're not butting in. I had almost given up asking you. I thought you knew that you were always welcome to go with us."

There was silence on his end again for a second. "Well, yeah, I sorta did know that. That's why I called."

I smiled, but I didn't laugh. "You riding over, or you want us to pick you up?"

He said he'd ride over, and when we went out to the car the next morning, there he was, all dressed up. When we picked up Cory, the redhead didn't seem to mind that Jimmy was with us. In fact, he seemed rather happy about it.

"You always come with them, Jim?"

"First time."

"Me too."

"I know."

They smiled at each other. It made me wonder if I would need to say anything later about what they heard in Sunday school and in the church service. Maybe I should just let them discuss it among themselves.

They were both quiet on the way home, until my mother asked them if they could stay for dinner. Both said they would have to call their moms, but my mother told them she already had and that it was all right.

At dinner I asked them what they thought of our Sunday school class. Jimmy was still quiet. Cory wasn't. "Your teacher is cool. Does he go to college?" I nodded. "And I liked the story. I want to hear how it ends."

That was good. "Does that mean you're coming again next week?"

"Can I?"

"Sure."

"Then, of course! Yeah. How 'bout you, Jim?"

Jimmy looked at Cory and shrugged. "Yeah, I guess. It was OK."

Cory kept jabbering. "When's that overnight camping trip with the cookout? Can I go on that, or do you have to be a real member of the class?"

I assured him he could come. "Anybody who comes to class is a member of the class."

"I'm comin' to that!" He looked at Jimmy again. "How 'bout you?"

"Nah. Camp-outs don't interest me."

I really wanted to know what they thought about what we learned that day, but I didn't want to push. "You'll come to Sunday school again next week though, right, Jimmy?"

He shrugged again and wouldn't look at me. "I'll think about it."

Jimmy is that kind of a guy. He wasn't going to make it too easy. I had invited him for two years, then he scolds me for planning to take Cory and not him. Then we go, and Cory loves it and wants to come back, and Jimmy is pretending not to care one way or the other.

Something told me that if Cory went, Jimmy would too. "OK, well, we know we'll be picking up Cory, and I guess we'll know if you're going if you're here at nine twenty-five, Jim."

He looked at me but didn't say anything. "I'm going to have to put a limit on the number of members of the sports club who can go with me, so if you know you can't go, let me know so I can give somebody else a chance."

I could tell by the look on Jimmy's face that he would be going. But still he didn't say anything.

9

Back to the Tournament

The next night I made sure the entire Baker Street Sports Club showed up at Jefferson High in plenty of time to see the whole game between the mighty Condors and the Hippos.

No one had said anything yet, but I think we all realized that even if we beat the Grenadiers later, we would then face the Condors, and it would be a matter of survival. The Condors looked as if they could beat a decent high school team.

I hadn't mentioned my encounter with Jack Bastable to any of the guys yet, and I watched and listened carefully to see what they might say about him during the semifinal. Mostly, they thought he looked mean, quiet, nasty. And like an excellent player.

For some reason, I couldn't figure out how he could be obviously retarded close up and yet be able to play with such quickness and gracefulness. He never spoke on the court, and when anyone spoke to him, he looked directly at them and appeared to be listening intently.

I watched especially when Petey Maxwell, the coach of the Condors, called the team together before the game started. He squatted and used a small magnetic replica of the court, moving little buttons around on it to represent the players from both teams.

Unless it was just my imagination, he seemed to speak more slowly and distinctly to Jack Bastable, and the big man scowled as he studied the diagram.

Then Coach Maxwell surprised me and everyone in the gym. He didn't start Bastable at center. He started a stocky, sandy-haired boy who was slow and whose face turned red as he ran up and down the court.

He always seemed to be behind the play. He pulled down a couple of rebounds in the first quarter and took three shots, making one. The one he made looked lucky to me. In fact, Brent and Toby looked back at me and rolled their eyes when his miracle shot banked in.

His other two shots were air balls and brought his coach up off the bench screaming at him. I still couldn't figure out why Bastable, the backbone of their team, wasn't playing.

All it did was make the Hippos look like stars. They outrebounded the Condors, and even though the Maxwell twins were shooting fairly well, any time they missed, the Hippos pulled down the ball and scored on a fast break.

The few times the Hippos had to take their time and set up a play, there wasn't the intimidating force in the center to con-tend with, so they just moved the ball around, keeping it away from the hands of the Maxwells, and eventually weaved it in to one of their front line, who scored over Bastable's substitute.

At the end of the first quarter, the Hippos led by twelve, but they looked defeated. They didn't have that hey-look-at-us-we-can-do-it look on their faces. They kept looking at the Condor bench and wondering when the big man would come sauntering in to turn the game around.

They didn't appear confident until the middle of the second quarter when they had built a twenty-point lead and it began to look like the Condors were not going to play Bastable at all.

The Hippos finally had the look of a team who felt it could whip its opponent. At least the opponent as it appeared on the floor at that time. And they could have.

The Hippos were a better team than they had shown in their boring win over the Falcons in the first round.

Without Bastable dunking shots over their center, clogging up the lane, making them force unnatural shots to get over him, and batting balls away, the Hippos played with poise. They were fast with quick and sure hands.

Their fundamentals were as sound as they had been in the first game. They made hardly any mistakes that resulted in turnovers, and suddenly I realized that we could play them for the championship if we got past the Grenadiers.

"Be watching the Hippos, boys. It may be time to quit studying the Condors."

Even though we had been in the league all of two days, we sensed the importance of the fact that the Condors were on the verge of losing their first game in more than two years. It seemed important, historic, yet somehow spoiled by the fact that Bastable was injured or sick. Or something.

Finally, with a minute to play in the first half, with the Condors trailing by twenty-four points, I saw Petey Maxwell kneeling in front of Bastable. The big man was concentrating hard, as if trying himself to figure out what the coach had been up to.

Maxwell called time, and Bastable replaced his substitute, who came to the bench huffing and puffing and flushed. The timeout wasn't quite over yet, and Coach Maxwell grabbed Bastable's arm, pulling him close for some last minute instructions. He also shouted something to the rest of the team.

It was Condors' ball out of bounds at the mid-court line. The pass went in to Bastable at the top of the key. He faked right and dribbled left, and as the defense converged on him in the middle, he stopped and hit a soft twelve-foot jumper.

He guarded the Hippo trying to throw the ball in, and I realized that for the first time in the game, the Condors had their famous full court press on. What was their coach trying to prove?

Bastable got a hand on the inbounds pass, grabbed the ball as it skipped away, dribbled once, and backed toward the basket for a stuff. The Hippos started to panic and threw the next inbounds pass high over Bastable's head out of bounds. The Condors fired it in to Mike Maxwell who alley-ooped a pass to the big man underneath.

He scored, and suddenly, within just ten seconds, the Condors had made up six points, all by Bastable. The Condors intercepted the next pass in, tossed the ball to the big man, and he faked a shot. The entire defense seemed to sag toward him, so he shoveled the ball out to Mickey Maxwell, the point guard, for an easy shot.

By the time the horn sounded for the end of the first half, the Hippos lead had been cut to four points. Bastable had scored twelve points, and the Maxwell brothers had combined for eight more. The Hippos had not had possession of the ball except out of bounds between plays.

It was the most dominating minute of basketball I had ever seen, including games on TV. Everybody knew that it was only a matter of time before the lead would be erased, the Hippos would be destroyed, and the Condors would win by virtually any score they wanted.

Would they keep that devastating full court press on the whole second half? It was just as grueling for the defense as for the offense, so it could wear them down. In a way, I hoped they would keep it on. If we were to have any chance at all to compete with them, it would have to be because they were a little worn out.

The only edge we had on them, and it was a small one, was that I thought we were in better shape, that we might have a little more endurance. Of course, if they played tomorrow like they were playing tonight, it wouldn't make any difference if we were marathon runners.

But what was I thinking about? We still had to beat the Grenadiers. And they were no slouches either. Watching the crazy Condor/Hippo game, I had nearly forgotten what to expect from our own opponent. I was still puzzling over what Petey Maxwell was doing.

Had he just been nice to the Hippos, letting them enjoy a regular game where they could run and pass and shoot without the big, dark, silent, nasty force of Jack Bastable on the court? Or was the coach showing off how he could let another team get two dozen points ahead and still pull that kind of power off the bench to turn the game around?

Deep down inside I had the feeling that what Maxwell had done was not good sportsmanship. He had not done it with the interest of the Hippos in mind. In fact, he had not done it in the best interest of his own team.

Certainly, it had not been good for Jack Bastable, even if his mind was slow enough to miss the point of it. He had to be somewhat embarrassed to be called upon to dominate and humiliate and embarrass a team like that, a team that had enjoyed building a lead that looked impossible to overcome.

No, I was convinced that Condor Coach Petey Maxwell had planned it all along to make himself look good. To show the Hippos and the rest of the league, especially the other two teams still in contention—the Grenadiers and the brand new Baker Street Sports Club—that there was virtually no beating this Condor club.

I had no idea how we could even keep from embarrassing ourselves in a game against them. I thought I heard Toby say he wished we would lose to the Grenadiers. Normally I would have hassled him about it and told him I didn't ever want to hear one of my teammates say anything like that. But he was our center. He would be the one trying to dribble through, pass around, and shoot over the big guy. I could hardly blame him if he wasn't looking forward to that.

The trouble was, we would have to play these guys more than once in the regular season anyway. So if it wasn't tomorrow night, it would be sometime. And as for me, I wasn't ready to just roll over and play dead for them.

Jimmy looked up at me from a couple of rows down and a few of the others looked too. "What're we gonna do if we win tonight, Dal?"

What was I supposed to say? "I'm working on it. Believe me, I'm thinking about it." And I was. A couple of strange thoughts were playing at my mind. Maybe some strategy.

Maybe something that could slow them down or somehow reduce their advantage.

I wasn't sure it would work, but it was something to think about. By the end of the game, which the Condors won by twenty, letting up at the end and sitting Bastable out again, I had decided that there were things we could try.

I thought we might be able to at least make a Baker Street/Condor game interesting. It would mean some emergency strategy sessions in the hayloft. I wasn't ready to think we had a chance at beating the Condors, but I certainly wanted the chance to face them.

That meant we had to get past the Grenadiers first.

10

The Semifinal

What a game! The Condors had dressed after their victory and sat behind the Grenadier bench, shouting encouragement to their old friends. I don't think the Condors cared much which team they faced in the final; they were that tough and confident.

I thought it was interesting that without Jack Bastable, even with the Maxwell twins playing guard, the Condors would have lost to the Hippos. That meant the rest of their team was not as impressive as it had been the last two straight years.

Our game against the Grenadiers was one of the most even games I've ever seen, let alone played in. They scored first, we tied them. Then they missed a shot, and we scored. They tied us. It went that way all through the first half. Neither team led by more than two points.

Even though the game was only half over, the fans were hoarse from screaming. Neither team was very sharp on the fundamentals. I guess we were all tired. But even with the turnovers and steals and missed shots, we just kept tying the game, back and forth.

I put Cory and Brent in again at the start of the third quarter. This time, Jimmy Calabresi looked grateful for the rest. Cory played tough defense again, but Brent had trouble stopping the bigger Grenadiers.

At the beginning of the second half, due to a couple of nice long shots by Cory, we finally went ahead by four. I almost relaxed. It seemed as if we could just break free of them, we could take off and win. They didn't seem that tough, but they frustrated us by always staying close.

Suddenly, there was a twelve-point swing. They made four shots from the field and four more from the free throw line, and we didn't hit a thing. We had gone from up by four to down by eight in about three minutes.

I saw panic on Cory's face. At first, it seemed to help him. He didn't want to lose, that was clear. He dived after loose balls, played defense so tight that he came close to fouling several times, and rebounded with such ferocity that I thought he'd hurt somebody, maybe himself.

When the referee called a charging foul on him, Cory slammed the ball on the court and it bounded high over the backboard. The ref called a technical foul, and Cory's face was crimson. He said something under his breath, and the referee tucked the ball under his arm and faced Cory.

"What did you say, son?"

"Nothin'!"

"That's a good idea, because if you get another technical, you're gone."

"You missed the call, ref!"

"That's fine. You can say your piece. But don't say what I thought I heard you say, or you're history."

"All right! I heard you, ref, OK?"

"Careful, son."

"All I said was that you're a —"

I ran over and threw my arms around Cory. "We've only got seven players, man! We don't need you getting thumbed out of the game."

"He's a jerk!"

"Don't let him hear you say that. You're wrong anyway. He's doing a good job. Take a break and have Jimmy come back in for you."

Cory turned on me. "You're a jerk too! I quit!"

He stormed off. I called time.

The ref disagreed. "You can call time after the free throw and the technical have been shot. Not before."

I ran off the court and caught Cory as he headed toward the locker room. "Don't say anything, Red. Just listen. You can quit after the game if you want. And maybe the rest of us will want you to. But you can't quit now, not in the middle of a tough game. We need you, and you'll really be letting us down. Nobody in the Baker Street Sports Club quits. If you're not on the bench when time is in again, you'll never play on another of our teams."

I ran back to the court while the second free throw was dropping through the net to give the Grenadiers a ten-point lead. Then the timeout began. I told the Baker Street boys we could win the game. "Their lead is a fluke. It just got away from us a little. We're better than this. Let's not try to get it all back at once. Be patient. Let's work the ball to Jimmy—and Jimmy, you get it in to Toby if you're not clear. Brent, I'm sorry, but I'm bringing Bugsy back in."

The whistle blew, and we were back on the court. I looked at the bench. Cory sat there with his head down. The Grenadiers scored again, and with four minutes left in the period, we were down by twelve. After having been even with them the whole game, we were blowing it.

"We were down ten-zip in the first game! Let's go Baker Street!"

Bugsy bounced a pass to me. I shoveled it out to Jimmy. He pulled up to shoot and was double-covered by the Grenadiers unusual offense. Jimmy lofted a pass to Toby, and our big man banked in a shot.

I signaled for a half-court press defense. We just had to get the ball back several times to be close going into the fourth quarter. I just knew we could beat this team, good as they were. Jimmy faked a pass back to me the next time down the court and then shot. He smiled sheepishly as the ball dropped through, knowing it was lucky. That was all right with me. We needed a little luck just then.

We came within six by stealing the ball and having Bugsy drive the lane for a lay-up. I was fouled while shooting, and

73

the ball went through the hoop, so my free throw would have brought us to within three. But I missed it. Actually, that was lucky, because Toby leaped and put through the rebound as the buzzer sounded.

As he came down, Toby landed on the foot of a Grenadier. Toby collapsed to the floor, writhing in pain, his ankle swelling as we watched. We would go into the fourth quarter down by just two, but Toby was in the locker room getting his ankle iced.

I moved Jimmy to center, even though he really wasn't tall enough or fast enough for the job. Then I had to choose between Brent and Cory for Jimmy's forward position. I didn't think we could win with Brent there. Maybe he could play guard, and I'd move Bugsy to forward. Nah. That would never work.

We slumped on the bench as the Grenadiers looked relieved. Their big lead had been cut down to next to nothing, but our center was out of action, and they knew we had a small bench.

Cory pleaded with me to let him play. "I'll be good, Dallas. Honest I will. I was just mad. I know I was wrong. Let me make it up to you and the team."

"Well, we're still going to have to talk about what you did."

"I know, but give me a chance to make up for it."

I wasn't sure I was doing the right thing, but I let him play. "We have to get the ball in to Jimmy. And Jimmy, you'd better play a high post, out away from the basket. They'll smother you underneath."

Cory seemed hesitant to shoot, but he was his usual self on defense and rebounding and passing. It took us a minute to get used to our new lineup, and the Grenadiers went ahead by four. Soon we settled down and quickly tied them up.

The rest of the fourth quarter went the same way the first half had gone. Back and forth, tied and untied, up by two, down by two. Both teams were exhausted, yet we raced up and down the court at full speed, trying anything that would turn the game in our favor.

The Grenadiers had the ball and a two point lead with thirty seconds to go, but Cory stole the inbounds pass and fed it to Ryan, streaking past. He scored to tie the game, but now the Grenadiers had the ball and a chance to win with twenty seconds to go. We had to stop them without fouling them.

We did neither. Cory fouled one of their shooters, and I was afraid he would explode. But he was mad only at himself. The Grenadier sank both free throws, and we were down by two with ten seconds left.

Cory took the inbounds pass the length of the floor and scored for the tie. The Grenadiers called timeout with two seconds on the clock. I figured they would either try a miracle shot or just tie up the ball and go into overtime.

I didn't think we could stand another quarter. They would have outlasted us because we didn't have enough substitutes. But when they tried throwing the ball in, Bugsy leaped and snagged it out of the air. He fired a desperation shot from about twenty-five feet, and we had won.

Whether we had enough strength left to even show up against the Condors, we didn't know.

By the time we left for the big game Tuesday night, so much had happened that my head was swimming. The club had met to decide whether we should give any punishment to Cory for his behavior in the semifinal. The answer was no, because his attitude made it appear that he was sorry.

Toby's ankle was strained but not sprained, and he was able to suit up. He would hobble around the bench during the game but would not plan on playing.

I had spent every other minute plotting strategy, and I hate to admit it but I even secretly scribbled a few notes about it during my classes at school. During study period I really got into it, writing down secret assignments for each player.

We were tired, there was no doubt about that. I couldn't believe we would have to face the best team in the league with a makeshift lineup and without a real center. Jimmy had done a decent job in relief of Toby, but something told me that lineup wouldn't work against Jack Bastable.

Finally, I had my plan all scoped out. The guys weren't so sure about it, but they agreed to try it. Bugsy spoke for all of them. "It's our only hope. It sounds crazy, but even if it doesn't work, everyone will know we tried."

The newspaper carried a story about the tournament, basically predicting a big victory for the Condors but also pointing out that there was a surprising new entry in the league that had somehow worked its way into the final. The Jefferson High gymnasium was full, even the balconies.

In the consolation game, the Hippos ran over the ex-hausted Grenadiers by twenty points. The Hippos played the way they had when Jack Bastable was on the bench. Just after the fourth period started, I took the Baker Street Sports Club into the locker room to dress for the game and to go over last minute instructions.

Toby wished he could play. I reminded him that he had his assignment, but he wanted me to go over it again.

"OK, at just the right time, maybe five minutes before tip off, you make your way over to their bench and talk to Coach Petey Maxwell. Tell him that your captain has been saying that the Condors wouldn't dare keep Bastable on the bench against Baker Street the way they did against the Hippos. No way."

"That's it?"

"That's it." He hobbled out.

The rest of the guys listened intently as I reminded each of his responsibility. Finally, I thought I saw that spark, that look on the faces of the five other guys that showed they really thought they could do it.

Not that they could win, but that they could pull off the plan I had designed and at least show the Condors that we were going to give it all we had. If we just waltzed out there and let the Condors take control of the game, I knew as well as my teammates did that there was no way we could stay with them.

11
The Final

C ory would start at center and would play ferociously—within the rules, of course—against Bastable or whatever Condor center was in the game. Jimmy and I would be at forwards with Ryan and Bugsy at guards.

"Let's not let our tiredness get to us. We can rest until next week before the league season starts. Play it to the hilt until it's over. Let's go!"

We raced onto the court, but we didn't shoot. We just stood under our own basket with three basketballs between us. We paired off and began passing back and forth to each other, bounce passes, chest passes, lobs. The crowd buzzed, probably wondering if we had forgotten to take our warm-up shots. Even the Condors watched us.

Toby was by their bench, and I saw him talking to Coach Maxwell. I hoped the message had been delivered. The coach said something to Bastable, and the big man didn't look any too happy, so I could only hope he would be sitting out much of the first half again.

With a minute on the clock before the game would begin, we lined up at the free throw line and each took two shots. It was incredible. It worked like a charm. All our free throw practice paid off. Everybody but me made both shots. I missed the first but swished the second. I had been the last shooter, and I followed the guys to the bench.

"We're likely to get a lot of booing and catcalls from this, and a lot of pressure from the Condors. But remember, I've seen it done in lots of college games. It's perfectly within the rules, so don't let them get to you. If we get shamed out of it, we'll lose for sure.

Toby told me the conversation with Coach Maxwell had gone exactly as I had predicted. When Toby told him I said he wouldn't dare leave Bastable out of the game, the coach said he would just see about that. "Then he went straight to Bastable and told him he was going to do the same thing tonight he did last night, Dallas." I clapped.

When we lined up for the opening tip, Jack Bastable was on the bench. We let them have the opening tip and tried to steal it, but Mickey Maxwell fed his brother, Mike, who rimmed a shot that Cory rebounded.

Rather than wasting our energy with a fast break, we took advantage of the fact that the Condors did not set up in a full or half court press, and we casually worked the ball up the floor. We passed and passed and moved and weaved, and finally both Cory and Jimmy found themselves open. Cory had the ball.

He faked a shot, drawing Jimmy's defender, then backdoored the pass to Jimmy, who nailed it. Then we went into our own full court press. The Maxwell brothers were again able to get the ball in, but I was convinced it was luck and that the next time—or even the next several times—we could stop them.

I had been defending against the forward passing the ball inbounds, so I told the guys on the way down the court that I would be sagging back and double teaming one of the Maxwells and that no one should cover the inbounds passer.

They looked puzzled, but I knew they'd do what I said.

The Condors were a little rattled by the fact that it had taken a lucky pass to even get the ball up the court, and our defense played them tight. Their forward dribbled off his foot right into my hands, and I fed Ryan on a breakaway. He scored to make it 4-0.

Jimmy and Cory were eager. As soon as the ball dropped through, they were yelling at me. "When do we start the plan?"

I held up both hands. "One more bucket. Six-point lead. Patience."

The other Condor forward took the ball out this time, and it looked to me as if Mike Maxwell was the target. I ignored the inbounds passer and ran to double team him with Bugsy. We were all over him. He couldn't break free.

The other guys had their men covered, and I saw the forward look to the other Maxwell brother. I switched to him and double teamed him with Ryan. The whistle blew. The Condors had taken too long to inbound the ball, and it was awarded to us.

I sneaked a peek at Coach Maxwell. He had exploded off the bench, face red, veins bulging as he screamed at his team. "Bush league! Come on, girls! Run the play, run the play!"

I took the ball out and bounced a pass in to Cory who was charging through the lane. He went up with the shot. It caromed out, but I had stepped inbounds just in time to go up for the rebound. I had to reach behind me to get it, but I saw Jimmy alone in the corner.

I hit the floor, whirled, and passed out to him, and as the defense turned on him, he passed it back in to me for an easy short shot. I shouted. "That's it! Next time we get the ball, the plan is on!"

Again I double teamed whoever looked like he was going to receive the inbounds pass as the Condor center was trying to throw the ball in. He was already huffing and puffing, and since he was the third man who had been chosen to try to get the ball in, he was feeling the pressure.

The seconds ticked away, and he grew more tense. Petey Maxwell leaped to his feet. "Throw it in! Throw it in! No more turnovers!"

The center let fly. Mickey Maxwell tried to race under the ball at the midcourt line, missed it, lost his balance trying to chase it down, and wound up kicking it out of bounds at the far end of the court.

Petey Maxwell called time-out and yelled at his players as they trudged to the bench. Over on our side, I knelt in the middle of the Baker Street Sports Club and spoke only one sentence. "I wish we'd have been able to put in one more bucket before they put Bastable in."

Then I just watched through the guys' legs as Jack Bastable reported to the scorer's table. The Condors had played right into our hands. While it would have been better to see the big center stay on the bench until almost halftime like last night, we still had the lead we needed to trigger our plan.

We were whistled back onto the court. "Patience, guys! Remember, only an easy shot. Nothing else!" They looked excited.

Bugsy went to take the ball out, and Bastable was there to cover him. I immediately switched places with him and was just able to find Ryan before taking too long. Ryan dribbled out to the top of the key while the Condors warily watched him.

Bugsy set up to his right, a little closer to the basket but still more than fifteen feet out. I was within six feet of Bugsy, and Jimmy was on the other side of the court, directly across from Bugsy. Cory was at the free throw line, right in front of Ryan.

Ryan stood there dribbling, while none of the rest of us moved. The Condors set up, waiting for the move, the play, the drive that would take the ball near the hoop where Bastable could knock it away and start their fast break. But Ryan stood still, feet parallel, hunched slightly over the bouncing ball, protecting it from the defender who was between him and Cory.

When Ryan's defender finally approached him, he sprang into action and passed past him to Cory. The Condors thought a play was on, but as soon as they converged on Cory, he dished the ball out to me, and I tossed it back to

82

Ryan. He again stood there dribbling, and the crowd started to realize what we were doing.

Immediately the shouts of "Stall! Stall! Boo!" reverberated throughout the gym. But Ryan just kept dribbling. They charged him again, he passed to Bugsy, Bugsy lofted it over their heads to me, I passed it in to Cory. He sent it back the same way it had come, and Ryan wound up with the ball, walking slowly and dribbling lazily twenty-five feet from the basket.

Every time his defender got close, Ryan dished the ball off. Petey Maxwell was screaming from the sidelines, calling us chickens and a few other things. Then he instructed his sons to double team the ball, wherever it went. They went into a diamond and one, where four defenders create a box, and the extra man follows the ball.

With two men swiping at him, Ryan rushed a pass to Cory, and as he leaped to get it he was fouled from behind by Bastable. How I wished he hadn't been fouled! When Bastable had left his low post near the basket to go for the interception, Jimmy had slipped underneath the basket and was wide open.

If Cory had come down with that ball, he would have heard me yelling, "Back door!" and would have fed Jimmy for an easy shot. As it was, he made his free throw, and we led by seven when the Condors took another time out.

They pulled a nifty play to get the ball past our press, and I had to give them credit. Bastable found Mickey Maxwell, who came back for the ball and passed it back to big Jack as he stepped inbounds. He rifled a pass to Mike Maxwell, who scored their first and only basket of the first quarter.

We stalled the rest of the way to lead 7-2 going into the second period. Bastable stayed in the game, and except for a couple of fouls that cost us two points and another breakaway that cost us two more, we held the lead at the half, 7-6.

"We need more points, boys. We've got to pull Bastable away from the basket and work a back door or two."

83

Jimmy wasn't so sure. "If we stall the rest of the way, we'll win by one."

I disagreed. "They're good for a basket or two a quarter just by luck or our mistakes. I think it's going to take more points for us to win this."

The best thing we had going for us was the anger of Petey Maxwell. He was livid. His team was trailing. They were being made to look bad. And they could lose. He wasn't patient. He didn't have a plan. We had him, and them, on the ropes.

In the third quarter we finally sneaked the ball past their defense for an easy basket. Later in that same period, when Bastable moved up on Cory, both Jimmy and I slid in behind him. With three of us on him the Condors were more worried about his breaking free than keeping track of Bugsy, who sank a long bank shot.

It wasn't the kind of a shot we should have been taking in a serious stall like that, but when Bastable was neutralized, we had to take our chances. We were up 11-6.

Our full court press was working wonderfully, though I was dead tired. I substituted Brent for myself and rested while shouting instructions from the bench.

Going into the fourth quarter, the score remained the same. The Condors were frustrated and panicky. They didn't want to lose, not like that. We didn't particularly want to win that way either, but we had no choice.

Toby had noticed something from the bench. "You know, Dal, you don't have to wait until Bastable moves up to score on him. He seems to get bored and relaxes after we hold the ball for a minute or so. I think if Cory suddenly turned and drove on him, took the ball right to him, Bastable wouldn't be ready for him. If he goes up with Cory, Cory can pass it off. If he doesn't, Cory can score."

I thanked him, and we tried that in the middle of the fourth quarter after the Condors had scored on a stolen pass. We sat and sat on the ball, and I kept watching the big man. His arms dropped, and he rocked back on his heels.

I caught Cory's eye, and the next time I got the ball I

tossed it to him at waist level, and he burst toward the basket. Bastable nearly fell over backwards as Cory scored. I knew we couldn't do it again, but I also knew if we could keep our heads about us and keep our endurance, we had a chance at upsetting the Condors. With two minutes to play, we led 13-8.

Finally, Petey Maxwell came up with a plan. He had the Condors start fouling us on purpose. We'd make a free throw, and then they would somehow get the ball past our tired press for two points. We were dying, trying to hang on, tongues hanging out, panting.

With a minute to play it was 16-14, our favor, and they were intentionally fouling us every time down the floor. I replaced Bugsy with Toby, which looked like a ridiculous move, but Toby is a better free throw shooter.

He couldn't move well on the press, so they scored two more baskets, but each came after a pair of free throws, two by Toby and two by Jimmy. We led 20-18, and they were desperate.

Their best players were fouling out, and we seemed to get a second wind. I kept urging the guys to hang on, and suddenly the Condors were beaten. They couldn't get the ball up the court, and when they fouled us, we were making the shots.

The stall had worked. The mighty Condors had fallen. We won 25-18.